This is the jacket I wear in the snow.

This is the zipper

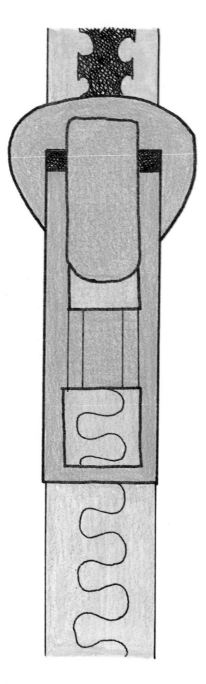

that's stuck on the  I wear in the snow.

This is the scarf, woolly and red,

that's caught in the

that's stuck on the  I wear in the snow.

This is the stocking cap for my head,

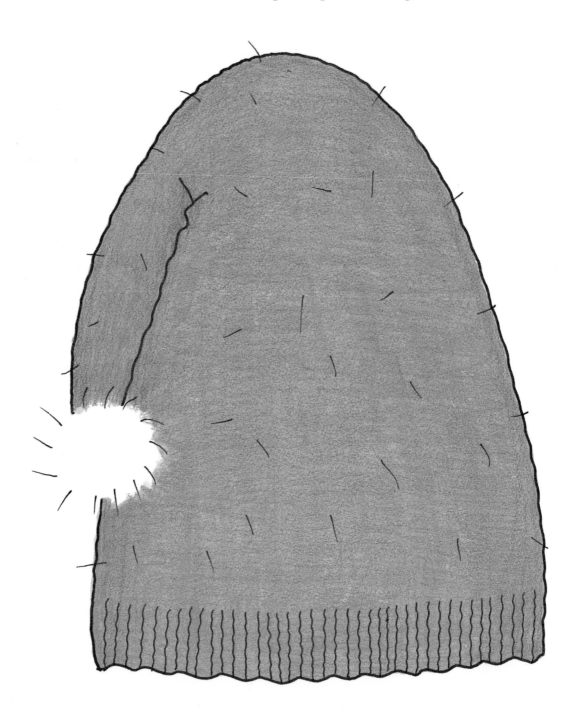

that matches the  woolly and red,

that's caught in the 

that's stuck on the  I wear in the snow.

These are the mittens that hang from each arm,

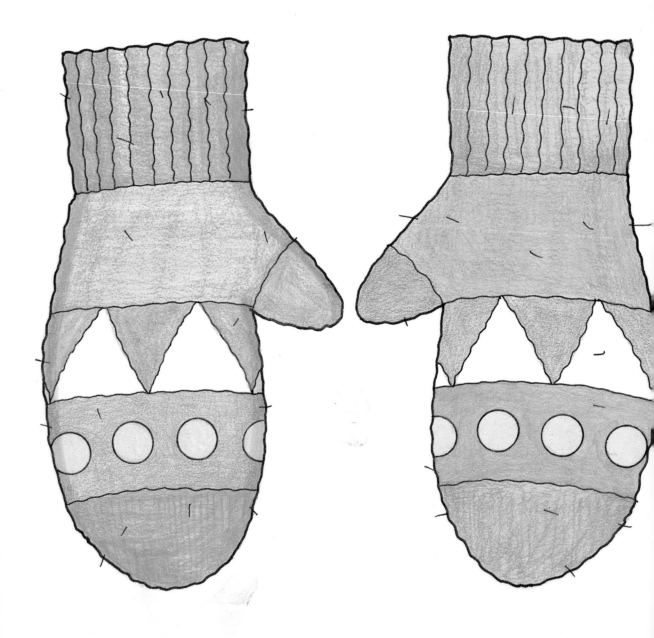

that I wear with the  for my head,

that matches the  woolly and red,

that's caught in the

that's stuck on the  I wear in the snow.

This is the sweater all itchy and warm,

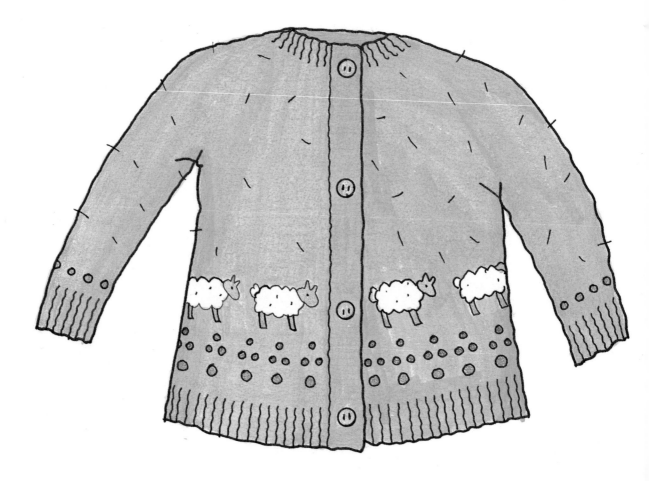

that meets the 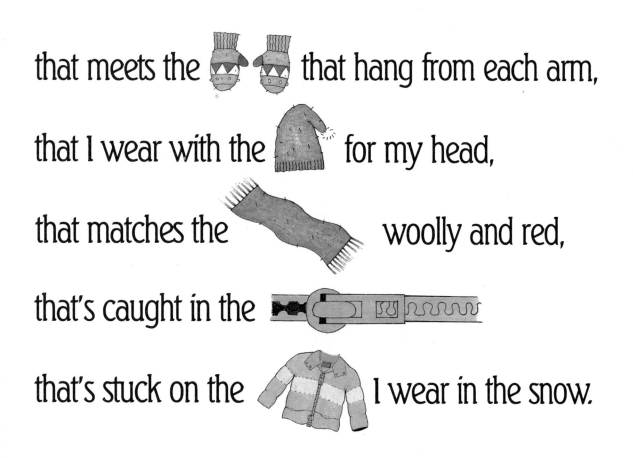 that hang from each arm,

that I wear with the for my head,

that matches the woolly and red,

that's caught in the

that's stuck on the I wear in the snow.

These are the jeans, stiff in the knee,

that go under the all itchy and warm,

that meets the that hang from each arm,

that I wear with the for my head,

that matches the woolly and red,

that's caught in the

that's stuck on the I wear in the snow.

These are the boots, too big for me,

that cover the  stiff in the knee,

that go under the all itchy and warm,

that meets the that hang from each arm,

that I wear with the for my head,

that matches the woolly and red,

that's caught in the

that's stuck on the I wear in the snow.

This is long underwear, bunchy and hot,

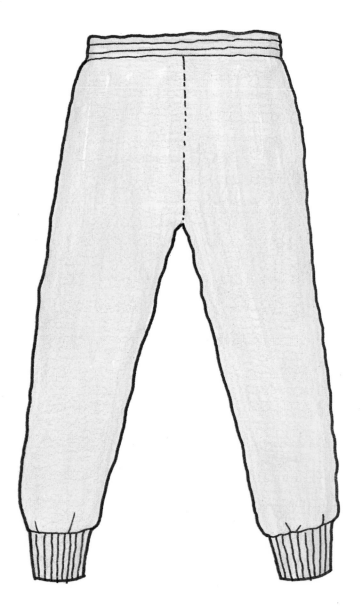

that is stuffed in the  too big for me,

that cover the stiff in the knee,

that go under the all itchy and warm,

that meets the that hang from each arm,

that I wear with the for my head,

that matches the woolly and red,

that's caught in the

that's stuck on the I wear in the snow.

These are the socks, wrinkled a lot,

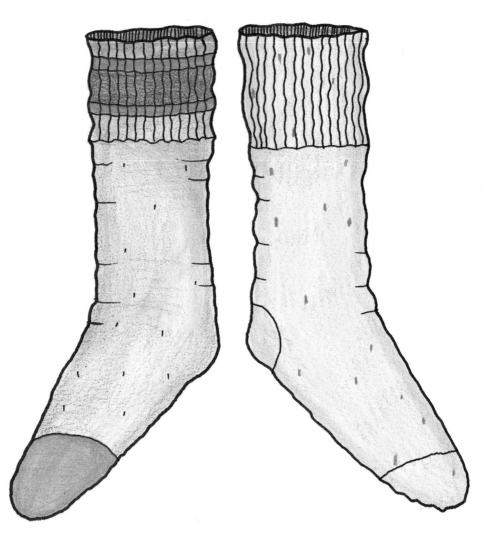

that are pulled over 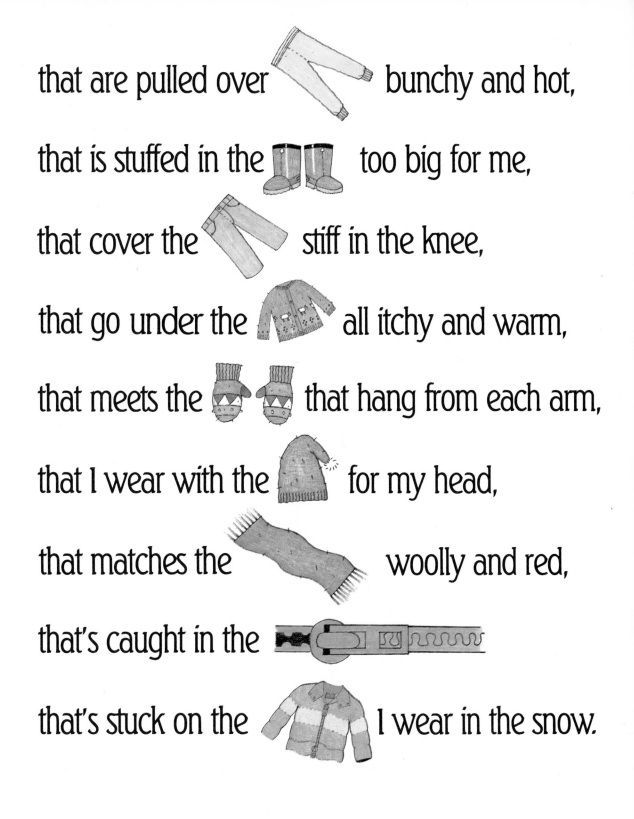 bunchy and hot,

that is stuffed in the too big for me,

that cover the stiff in the knee,

that go under the all itchy and warm,

that meets the that hang from each arm,

that I wear with the for my head,

that matches the woolly and red,

that's caught in the

that's stuck on the I wear in the snow.

These are the tears that fell from my eyes,

that dripped on the  wrinkled a lot,

that are pulled over bunchy and hot,

that is stuffed in the  too big for me,

that cover the stiff in the knee,

that go under the all itchy and warm,

that meets the that hang from each arm,

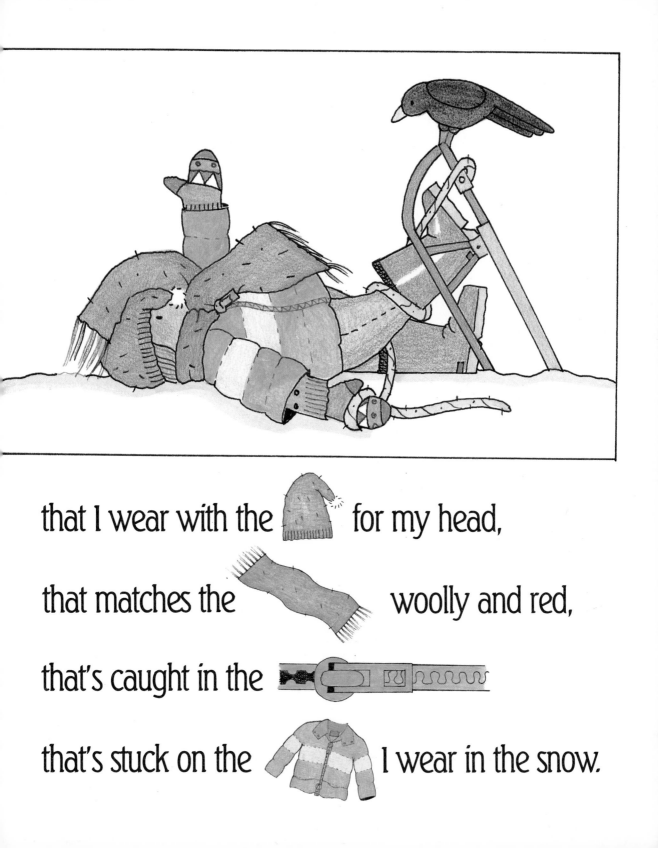

that I wear with the ![hat] for my head,

that matches the ![scarf] woolly and red,

that's caught in the ![zipper]

that's stuck on the ![jacket] I wear in the snow.

This is my mother, who heard my cries,
and wiped the tears that fell from my eyes,

and loosened the scarf, woolly and red,
and slipped off the stocking cap from my head,

and unpinned the mittens that hung from each arm,
and unbuttoned the sweater all itchy and warm,

and unzipped the boots, too big for me,
and straightened the jeans, stiff in the knee,

and smoothed the long underwear, bunchy and hot,

and pulled up the socks that were wrinkled a lot,

when she unstuck the zipper
of the jacket I wear in the snow.